Nathaniel Holmes Morison

**The captive and other early rhymes**

Nathaniel Holmes Morison

**The captive and other early rhymes**

ISBN/EAN: 9783337271701

Printed in Europe, USA, Canada, Australia, Japan

Cover: Foto ©Andreas Hilbeck / pixelio.de

More available books at **www.hansebooks.com**

# THE CAPTIVE

## AND OTHER EARLY RHYMES

BY

NATHANIEL HOLMES MORISON

PRIVATELY PRINTED

BALTIMORE

1888

# A Souvenir

## FOR MY CHILDREN.

### Fifty Copies Printed.

JOHN MURPHY & CO., PRINTERS,

BALTIMORE.

TO



---

*WITH THE KIND REGARDS*

*OF THE AUTHOR*

# CONTENTS.

1*

# 6                    *Contents.*

# SIDNEY, MY DEAR WIFE,

### THE BELOVED OF MANY YEARS.

*A gentle voice, a winning smile,*
    *A heart both soft and true;*
*A generous trust that knows no guile,*
    *A love forever new;*
*Devotion with unselfish aim*
    *To sweet domestic life;*
*Obedience swift to every claim*
    *Of sister, mother, wife;*
*A thoughtful care and tenderness,*
    *A courage ever sure;*
*Prudence and will without excess,*
    *And faith that will endure;—*
*These traits thy gentle life has shown*
*With grace and sweetness all thine own.*

1888.

# Introductory.

## INDEPENDENCE DAY.

This day a corner-stone was laid
    Of empire broad and grand ;
This day our fathers, undismayed
By tyrant's frown or hireling's blade,
For freedom and for country made

    A pledge of heart and hand ;—
A pledge of life and honor fair,
Of wealth and all that wealth can bear ;
A pledge of love which here bestows
The purest joy that manhood knows ;

Of home where gathers all we love,
Of peace, bright gleam of heaven above;—
    All these our fathers cheerful gave
    A country for their sons to save.
Hail then to each immortal name
That gleams upon that scroll of fame,
    The charter of our land !
All honor, all renown and praise
Upon these saints of other days !
And may the arch they sought to raise
    Forever stand,
Firm as the rocks that steadfast frown
O'er fair Monadnock's lofty crown.

    I turn from them, the noblest band
That ever guarded freedom's land,
Or freedom's guiding charter planned,
To other climes as fair and bright,
But scourged with dark oppression's blight.

# THE CAPTIVE.

## I.

The patriot's plaintive strain I sing,
When freedom's cause lay weltering
In blood the tyrant vainly shed,
To bind the crown upon his head;
When high on Europe's cheerless night
    A flaming meteor burst;
An instant, with its dazzling light,
To guide the traveller's steps aright,
To rouse his hopes, those hopes to blight,
    Then die a thing accursed.
Oh! did that power to me belong,
That, through the northern minstrel's song,
    Infused its strength divine,
I'd touch the lyre with fingers skilled,

Till every heart with horror thrilled,
And blood in coursing veins were chilled,
　　To hear a strain like mine.
Presumptuous thought! begone full soon;
For heaven will never grant the boon.


II.


But who can paint the dungeon's gloom,
Where sad the captive serves his doom,
Whom proud oppression's arm has torn
From friends that love and hearts that mourn?
Who can describe the brow sedate?
The heart all drear and desolate?
The listless eye that cannot trace
The wrinkles furrowed on the face?
The man whose ear no more retains
A knowledge of his clanking chains,
Nor heeds the sound of bolt or bar
That echoes through the vaults afar?
Who, buried in his dungeon deep,

Till all his senses seem to sleep,
Doth often raise his fading eye,
As if to view the azure sky,
Whose image years of fiendish art
Could never banish from his heart?
If such there be, his song should tell
The tortures of earth's deepest hell,
What captives long did think and feel
Immured within the French Bastille.

### III.

'Twas midnight, and the placid Seine
    Rolled darkly on its winding way;
Above the cloudless moon was seen;
    Below the troubled city lay,
Whose bright illuminating glare
Far on the stilly night did stare;
For lamp and torch did brightly gleam,
Contending with the moon's pale beam.
Along the glaring street was heard

2

The sentry's measured tread ;
The challenge hoarse and shrill watch-word
From angry lips the night wind stirred,
    And struck the heart with dread ;
And the clattering of wood-clad feet
Went sounding on through lane and street.


IV.


High frowning o'er the city bright,
    The lofty Bastille hung ;
Eight massive towers threw back the light
Of moon or torch, which o'er the night
    A radiant vesture flung ;
And soldiers, trained in guarded tent,
Pace slowly on the battlement,
And watch with fearful anxious eye,
The forms that glide in silence by ;
While round, in circling heaps afar,
Are piled the iron bolts of war.

## V.

The walls twice fifty feet arise,
    Thrice three in thickness they,
With deep broad ditch, their strength defies
    The flower of war's array ;
Yet ere to-morrow's setting sun,
This fortress shall be lost and won ;
Lost by a troop of warrior men,
Won by the infuriate citizen.

## VI.

Within that high and massive wall
    Is many a dreary cell ;
And many a tale that would appal,
Of murder's groan and mercy's call,
    Those gray old rocks might tell.
'Tis well their tongues kind nature sealed,
Or such dark tales had been revealed,
That man, a dreadful truth to know,

Had ceased to feel for human woe;
And yet, to show the captives' state,
One, only one, will I relate.


## VII.


Deep in his cell at noon of night,
    The lonely captive lay;
He knew not that the moon was bright,
Or that the city, bathed in light,
    Rivalled the orb of day.
Shut from the world, he lingered there,
A monument of blank despair;
Nor shining moon nor torches dim
Dispelled the gloom of night for him.
His eye had lost the sparkling fire
That youth and health alone inspire;
And, sunk within its socket deep,
Did yet its midnight vigils keep.
His hair was gray, his hand with age
Had withered in his dungeon cage.

One leg was gone, the other lay
Half-wasted by the damps away ;
But round his ankle even yet
The cruel fetters, firmly set,
Enchained the cripple, sad and sore,
Unpitying to the marble floor.
Filthy rags o'er wool flocks spread
Composed his only chair and bed ;
While stone above, beneath, around,
When seen at noontide, sternly frowned.
A grated window, high and small,
Placed deep within the massive wall,
Could only at the noon of day,
Admit a feeble struggling ray ;
But long ere day has winged its flight,
That cell is buried deep in night.


### VIII.


There on his bed with watchful eye
  The lonely captive lowly lay ;

2*

He often turned, and oft a sigh
　　To faint expression found its way ;
And fast adown his furrowed cheek
　　Tear after tear successive stole ;—
His manly purpose all too weak
　　To check the torrent's wild control.
He deemed that time and sorrow deep
　　Had dried the fountains of his heart ;
For long, long years he could not weep,
　　And grief to him had lost its smart.
Why sighs he then at midnight hour?
　　Why turns he thus from side to side?
Why feelings now resume a power
　　That long and dreary years denied?
Perchance, in dreams he seemed a boy,
　　Through meadows bounding wild and free ;
Perchance a man, and could enjoy
　　Once more the world's serenity.
Perchance he dreamed that time at length
　　Had turned the tyrant's heart of stone ;
With faded youth and wasted strength,

He trod the cold, wide earth alone,
And passed the crowd to all unknown,
    A stranger in his native land,—
No kinsman's eye to greet his own,
    No friend to grasp his withered hand.
So dreamed he, and the bitter tears
    Came streaming from his swollen eyes;
He sighed, awoke, suppressed his fears,
    And yet fond hopes of freedom rise.


### IX.


In youth, ere yet the fatal dart
Had pierced his young and gladsome heart,
And forced him from the world away,
To poison every future day,
He danced the fields of living green,
And roamed the banks of lovely Seine,
    A gay and reckless boy.
He claimed a father's tender care,
A mother's ardent love did share,

And pleasures pure, and visions fair,
    Did his young heart enjoy.
He loved the fields, the vine-clad hills,
And oft beside the tinkling rills,
That sung their merry course along,
Would sit for hours and list the song,
That seemed in tranquil waves to roll
Its notes through his enraptured soul.
The changing clouds, the stars, the wind
With him held converse, and his mind,
Now shattered by his wrongs and age,
Drank deep from many a classic page.
His taste was pure, his feelings told
They came from nature's finest mould;
His heart, so soft yet stern to dare,
It seemed that naught was wanting there;
Sweet music in his soul did lie;
The poet sparkled in his eye;
A nation's heart he bore along,
And chained enraptured to his song.
Even now, to the admiring stage,

He seemed the Shakspere of his age;
Even now his fickle country smiled
On him as her most gifted child.
His hopes were high, his visions bright,
Too soon, alas! to set in night.


X.


The glow of youth had passed, and now
The sun of manhood lit his brow.
He saw his country faint and bleed,
Like a hard-spurred, far-ridden steed.
With bitter tears he mourned the day
She owned the Bourbons' iron sway,
Nor sought, though fond of peace and rest,
To lock the feeling in his breast.
His country's wrongs did thus inspire
His hand to touch the tuneful lyre;
He struck a chord whose plaintive tone
Seemed but the nation's stifled moan.
Now high, now low, with that sad wail

Did breasts responsive rise and fail.
As when the heart, with anguish wrung,
Supplies a prayer and prompts the tongue
To speak; now the sound of bitter woe
Is choked with sobs; now faint and low
Is heard; then, bursting all restraint,
It pours a loud and sad complaint.
So rang that lyre; its early strain,
So low and sad, did scarce complain;
But, as it rolled its notes along,
More earnest grew the plaintive song,
Until it seemed in waves to roll
Its moanings through the human soul.

### XI.

So rang that lyre, yet few were they
Who listened to its mournful lay;
For soon its strain, now pitched so high,
Has caught the censor's watchful eye,
And never more will lips of men

Repeat those pensive notes again.

His works proscribed, himself they brand

As traitor to his native land ;—

That land his heart had loved so well!

That land for which he fain would sell

His birthright! yea, would drain his veins,

Or brave a dungeon's cruel chains!

That land whose wrongs had fired his soul!—

To her a traitor! to enroll

His name with theirs, the base,

The vilest of the human race!

This was the bitter thought that stung

    His soul with pain severe;

And this the piercing sound that rung

    Forever in his ear.

Compared with this, the clank of chains

Had been the minstrel's merry strains;

Compared with this, the rack, I say,

Had turned his heart from grave to gay;

The gibbet been a welcome name;—

He only wished a spotless fame.

### XII.

He loved his country, and he wept
The wrongs 'neath which she tamely slept ;—
This was his crime.   For this they tore
His heart from all it loved before ;
From kindred, friends, the earth, the skies ;
From man and human sympathies.
For this, pronounced his hapless doom,
And shut him in a living tomb.
For this they made him wear a chain ;
For this his honor sought to stain ;
For this, insult ; for this, deny
The wretched pleasure even to die,
But bid his life-blood still to flow,
And still prolong his ceaseless woe.

### XIII.

In summer when the fields were clad
In verdure, and all nature glad ;

And when from morn till eve of day,
The songster poured his merry lay,
    They shut him in his cell;
And many a summer came and went,
And songsters' lively strains were spent,
But on his ear, in dungeons pent,
    No living voices fell.
He heard no more the lips of men,
And every sound by hill and glen
    Had bid his soul farewell.
. Mute was the slave, that, morn and eve,
His scanty crust and broth did leave;
Mute was the smith, who, thrice each sun,
His chains examined one by one,
And mute the sentry evermore
Pacing along the corridor.
No human voice that silence broke;
But the walls answered when he spoke.

### XIV.

Thus years rolled on, but left no trace
To tell their flight, save that his face
Was stamped with many a furrow deep,
And that his eyes forgot to weep.
Still wept his heart; still sighed he low,
Though the salt tears refused to flow.
He learned at length to rest, with head
Unpillowed, on his marble bed ;
He learned to hear his clanking chain,
Nor feel his bosom pierced with pain ;
He learned to crave his wretched food,
To love his dungeon's solitude.

### XV.

He saw the harmless insects crawl
Upon the loathsome prison's wall,
And felt, beneath that vault of stone,
Though lonely, he was not alone.

Those insects ever creeping there
Did all his warm affections share.
To them his food he oft did lend;
The spider soon became his friend;
The timid mice came forth to play,
And skipped about right merrily.
He watched their capers, and forgot
The sorrows of his hapless lot;
Forgot his chain, the bolted door,
And all the wrongs he felt before;
He seemed a moment free, and then
Sad, sickening thoughts returned again.

## XVI.

Thus years rolled on; no changes came;
His sighs, his pastimes all the same;
And still untried, unsentenced there,
He lay deep buried in despair.
Three lustrums he had worn his chain,
And life's dark sun began to wane,

The visions of his youth had fled,
And hope's last lingering spark was dead,
When night enclosed the world once more,
And he, flung loosely on the floor,
Was wrapped in sleep; and lo! a light
Streamed through his cell intensely bright.
Its sudden flash and dazzling beams
Awoke the sleeper from his dreams.
He leaped the window high to gain,
And frantic broke the heavy chain
That bound his limbs; then summoned all
His strength to scale the naked wall;
But vain his efforts; block or stone
To aid his ascent there were none.


XVII.


Now from the prison far and near,
Loud cries of fire! fire! reached his ear.
The guard cried as he left his post,
O! Blessed Virgin, we are lost!

And voices never heard before
Resounded through the corridor.
He list those sounds with strange delight,
Though filled with horror and affright;
For since captivity began
He scarce had heard the speech of man;
And every tone his ear did greet
Like the soft notes of music sweet.


XVIII.


He listened, and he knew the flame
From the vast pile of the Bastille came;
For he heard along the prison's side,
As one voice spoke and one replied.
"While thus the flames our strength defy,
Shall these 'caged birds' be left to die?
To waste in cells to ovens turned?
To be by lingering torture burned?"
"The rules are strict," the other said,
"To transgress is to lose my head;

3*

And yet I would not see them burn,
Though bar or bolt I dare not turn.
Speed thou for life, for mercy speed,
To gay Versailles on fleetest steed,
And bring me from our gracious King,
A warrant sealed with signet ring.
For life, for death thou must wait
Or thou shalt rue the captives' fate."
"I go," said he, "though death I meet,"
And the walls echoed to his feet.


XIX.


The captive heard, his heart was chilled,
And every vein with horror thrilled;
For grim, pale death, in ghastliest guise,
Glared on him with his stony eyes,
And clenched his fists, and, fierce and grum,
He seemed to howl, "I've come, I've come."
For years the captive's voice arose
In prayer for death to end his woes;

But his heart shrunk with instant fear,
To see the pale monster standing near,
And he listened every sound that came,
To learn the progress of the flame.
And now the tumult seems to rise,
And now a single moment dies;
Now bursts again upon his ear;
And now a voice he seems to hear.
"Can it be his," he eager cried,
"Who late to gay Versailles did ride?"
Yes, no, his beating heart rejoined,
And calmed the transports of his mind.

## XX.

An hour has passed; he hears no more
The tumult through his bolted door;
The light has left his gloomy cell;
Each voice has bid his ear farewell;
And, save the sentry's solemn round,
Dread silence reigns in gloom profound.

The captive laid his aching head
Once more upon his lonely bed;
But spectres, through the gloomy night,
No longer stalked before his sight.
His weakness now he saw with pain,
Regretted the extinguished flame,
Since it had left him thus again,
A victim in the hands of men.
A long, sad, sleepless night he passed,
But the dull morning dawned at last.
The smith renewed his chains once more,
And days rolled on as they rolled before.

## XXI.

Since morning closed that gloomy night,
Three lustrums more have winged their flight;
And, lo! the captive, still in chains,
Endures the rack of sterner pains.
His mind, by long afflictions torn,
Had every injury calmly borne,

While yet he deemed that heaven above
Sustained him with eternal love;
But such fierce anguish wrings his brow,
He deems himself deserted now;
And this dark thought disturbed more,
Than all the wrongs he felt before.


XXII.


A tumor, armed with pains severe,
   Had clasped his withered knee,
His mind, oppressed with gloomy fear,
   Was sunk in misery.
Erect no more, his hoary head
He laid upon his prison bed.
Distressed, alone, with every breath,
He breathed a silent prayer for death;
Or cursed with impious lips the day
That smiled upon his birth so gay.

## XXIII.

Thus days passed on, no soothing balm
Was brought his burning pains to calm ;
No friend was near to dress the limb,
Or speak a cheering word to him.
The pains increased, from day to day
The putrid flesh did fall away,
Until he deemed each sun that rose
Would bring an end to all his woes.
But still its beams did morning give,
And still he did not cease to live.

## XXIV.

At length a surgeon came ; but he,
Well versed in human misery,
Was forced to wipe the bitter tears
From eyes that had not wept for years.
He bade the smith remove the chain,
And sought to soothe the captive's pain

By all the means his art supplied.

With warmest hope and zeal he tried

To save life's taper, flickering dim,

But could not save the sickly limb.

He bade the sufferer then prepare,

The pain of severed nerves to bear;

And, when the King's consent were known,

He would remove the aching bone;

For even this required to be

Confirmed by such authority.

The King had left Versailles, and fast

To the far distant South had passed.


XXV.


Eight weary days the captive lay,

And bore the pangs of slow decay;

Eight weary days, with constant care,

The surgeon sat beside him there,

And sought, with all a Christian's zeal,

To soothe the pain he could not heal.

The captive's heart, so sad and sore,
Oppressed with all the wrongs he bore,
Now melts, and tears bedew his eye,
To meet with human sympathy.
His lips, that lately breathed a curse
On God, mankind, the universe,
Now move in prayer, and now in praise
To God, the author of his days.
His mind relieved and calmed again,
He scarcely deemed his knee a pain,
So light were now the pangs he bore,
Compared with those he felt before.


### XXVI.


And when the mandate came, he knew
That doubtful was the breath he drew;
For the heavy door was opened wide,
And in a hoary priest did stride,
Who spoke of death, of suffering,
And many another holy thing.

To all he said the captive list,
Received the offered eucharist,
And, when the holy man was gone,
And he was in his cell alone,
He raised to heaven an earnest prayer,
To end his life and sorrows there.
But heaven had doomed him still to sigh
For years, and then unbound to die;
In the free air to meet with death,
Untainted by a dungeon's breath.


XXVII.


And soon the skilful surgeon came,
To part the members of his frame;
He soon divided flesh and bone;
Soon tied the arteries one by one;
Soon the ice and bands applied;
And soon he staunched the purple tide.
Nor did the captive loud complain,
But bore unheard the subtle pain,

4

Until the limb was borne from view,
When sighing he but said adieu,
And swooning dropped upon the bed,
Which late the attendant gaoler spread;
For his pillow was a stone before,
His only bed the oaken floor.
Forty long days in pain he passed,
And, lo! the wound is healed at last;
And the smith has come to clench the chains
Around the ankle that remains.


### XXVIII.

Three lustrums more have passed away;
'Tis midnight's lonely hour, I say;
    The captive now doth weep.
In dreams he roamed the fields once more,
And listened to the water's roar,
And saw the friends he loved before;
    But, when aroused from sleep,
He found the dungeon still his home,

Nor heard the waters leap and foam,
Nor saw the fields he loved to roam,
And, see, like rain the big tears come,
    And down in torrents sweep;
For many a vision dark and bright
Come thronging o'er his faded sight,—
Fair, youthful scenes, in age's night
    Still stamped on memory deep.
And thus the silent tears do seek
To drench the captive's furrowed cheek.


## XXIX.


'Tis morn; the earth the bright sun greets,
And Paris, through her crowded streets,
    A living tide doth pour.
No power can now its course control,
As waves on waves successive roll,
    Each swelling more and more.
From every building close or wide,
Gushes forth the angry tide;

While lashing round the Bastille's side,
    The torrents chafe and roar.
No hand can now avert thy fate,
Thou earth-born hell, at last, though late,
    Thy towers are doomed to fall;
For, lo! a nation raised to life,
Each heart with direful vengeance rife,
In clamorous shouts the deadly strife
    For thy destruction call.
So loud each shout, so fierce each yell,
It seemed that every fiend in hell
    Had been in upper air;
Yet not a voice of all we hear
Hath reached the captive's eager ear,
    Or pierced a dungeon there.


### XXX.


'Tis noon, and still collects the throng;
Still rush the mighty waves along;
Still lash against the Bastille's side,

And bounding echo far and wide,

    In wild tumultuous roar.

An hour has passed, the bell strikes one,

That in the central tower has hung,

    For ages three or more;

And now from window, roof, and street,

Flames burst in many a fiery sheet;

Volley on volley in the heat

    Of burning rage they pour;

And groans and shouts terrific meet,

    The troubled city o'er.

The balls, like rain-drops, strike the wall,

Then harmless to the earth do fall;

'Midst flame and smoke the towers on high

Look down in fearless majesty.

On, on the maddened people come,

Nor banner gleams, nor pealing drum

    Directs their hasty feet;

And louder still the shouts arise,

Missile on missile swiftly flies,

And muskets flame athwart the skies,

4*

Soldiers and people meet.
Stern death through all the conflict flies,
    Her bloody feast to greet.


## XXXI.


But hark! the earth shakes 'neath the tread,
And deafening peals of thunder dread
    The lowest dungeons hear;
For now the Bastille's cannons spread
    Destruction far and near.
Dyed deep in gore of martyrs dead,
High waves a flag of bloody red
    Upon a pointed spear;
Each softer passion now has fled;
    Vengeance alone is dear.


## XXXII.


But see, amid the deadly strife,
Where angry passions sport with life,

A helpless maid is borne along,
Sustained by an insulting throng.
" De Launay's daughter, he whose sway
Is o'er the Bastille's walls to-day,"
    Loud ruffian voices cry ;
" Let the child answer with her life,
The father's conduct in the strife,"
    Ten thousand tongues reply.
And now to where bright flames of red
Shoot from many a burning bed,
    The helpless maid they bear ;
But ere they reach this awful pyre,
A youth, before whose glance of fire
The mob on either side retire,
    Shakes his bright sword in air.
With angry look and panting breath,
Snatching the hapless maid from death,
    He cries, " By heaven, I swear,
If one this lovely virgin harm,
He falls 'neath my avenging arm ;
His life blood, oozing fresh and warm,

The thirsty earth shall share."
Thus loud he spoke, and his dark eye,
In stern resolve, flashed fearfully.
The ruffians quail beneath his brand,
Fixed the astonished people stand,
And learn the maiden has no claim
To proud De Launay's hated name.


XXXIII.


The clock strikes five; the whirlpool's rage
Around the captive's rock-built cage,
   Is fiercer than before.
The drawbridge falls with thundering crash;
On, on the maddened people dash;
Falchions gleam, and muskets flash,
   And treble thunders roar;
Axes on massive portals clash;
   The streets o'erflow with gore.

### XXXIV.

The summons once, and yet again,
De Launay heard with high disdain;
But now, compelled by urgent fate,
He yields reluctant, but too late
   A frightful death to shun;
He opes the tottering portals wide,
In rushes fast the living tide,
And shouts the tiring breezes ride;
   The Bastille dread is won.
Low bows the monarch's cherished pride,
   And sets his golden sun.


### XXXV.

The captive heard the cannon's peal,
   That shook the massive pile;
He heard the thundering clash of steel
   Against the gates, the while;
And now he hears the deafening din,

Of men and arms the walls within;
He hears them rush with shouts along;
He hears the blows of hammers strong;
He feels his rock-built prison shake;
He sees the heavy hinges break,
The massive bars of iron crush,
And in his brave deliverers rush.
They snatch him from his chains away,
And bear him to the light of day.
Strange thoughts and feelings undefined
Came crowding o'er his feeble mind.
His midnight dreams by day fulfilled
Seemed but a warning heaven had willed.
Exhausted nature could no more
Support the weary load he bore;
He only asked the sun to see;
He saw,—and died in ecstacy.

## XXXVI.

Such is the captive's tale so rudely sung,

Such the deep wrongs his gentle bosom stung;

Such one dread echo from that cage of stone;

Such the foul caverns 'neath the glittering throne.

Would you learn all the captive's tale of woe,

Read Silvio's Prisons, Maroncelli know;

And do you still his name and kindred ask,

Read then the sufferings of the Iron Mask.

1838.

## UNION VILLAGE.

### A FAREWELL.

Farewell to Unionville,
   Farewell to all that's there;
I go but shall remember still
   The joys I once did share.
In thee I laid my boyish schemes
   To act in after life,
While playing by thy beauteous streams
   Unknowing care or strife.
But now those days have passed away,
   And I can here no longer stay.

How oft I've wandered far and near
   Upon thy lovely hills;
How fair those woody steeps appear,
   To hearts unvexed by ills;

But fairer still and lovelier yet
   Thy silvery waters glide,
Whose sparkling gleams, like pearls in jet,
   I've watched with boyish pride.
But I must take my parting view,
   And bid these beauteous scenes adieu.

In thee I've spent my happiest days,
   My boyhood's gayest hours,
And now I can but sing thy praise,
   When parting from thy bowers.
My breast sweet recollections fill,
   How through thee I did roam,
And knew thee, lone and lovely vill,
   As boyhood's happy home.
But now I hear the parting knell,
   So once again farewell, farewell.

Peterboro', 1833.

## TO AGNES.

Fair lady, now I bid farewell
  To one whose worth I know;
On thee my thoughts will often dwell,
  When far away I go;
Thy virtues for a guide I'll take,
  When I'm beset with ill;
Our friendship formed for friendship's sake,
  Shall be for friendship still;
And, though I roam o'er land and sea,
My heart shall ever cling to thee.

That gentle voice, so often heard
  Like music soft and sweet;
The pleasant smile, the cheering word,
  That did my coming greet;

That heart to soft emotions kind,
 Those hands so swift to move;
That sweetness, grace, and truth, combined
 With tenderness and love;—
Oh! these shall ever with me stay,
Roam o'er the world where'er I may.

PETERBORO', 1833.

## ACROSTIC.

As the compass and chart, when the storm winds
    are raging,
Guide safely the ship o'er the dark rolling brine;
Not otherwise virtue, calm, sweet, and engaging,
Each pleasure enhancing, each sorrow assuaging,
Shall guide you securely with wisdom divine.

PETERBORO', 1834.

## ACROSTIC.

May the eve of thy life be as calm and serene,
As its morning is cheerful and gay;
Roll back, ye dark clouds, that would cover the
    scene;
Ye pleasures, be kindly and stay.

PETERBORO', 1834.

# FOR AN ALBUM.

### James Green.

I write not here to please each eye,
  That chances o'er these leaves to stray,
Whose stranger glance, in hurrying by,
  Stays but to criticise my lay.
No critic eye my lines invite,
  Stranger, for thee I do not write.

I write not here the world to tell,
  That I have drunk Castalia's spring,
Have seen Parnassus' summits swell,
  And heard the vocal muses sing.
Oh ! that such claims were truly mine,
  The muse should breathe in every line.
5*

I write not here to gather fame,
  Or bind the laurel round my head ;
I write not to preserve my name,
  When life with all its joys has fled.
No! purer motives tune my lyre,
  And all its friendly themes inspire.

For I do write, my friend, for thee,
  That, when thou dost peruse my rhymes,
Thy thoughts may far, far backward flee,
  To other scenes and other times.
Should they recall our youth again,
  Oh! then I have not writ in vain.

I write that, when long years have fled,
  And cares and sorrows choke thy way,
When early hopes and schemes are dead,
  Thou then may'st read my youthful lay;
May'st drop a tear on friendship's shrine,
  And claim once more a thought of mine.

EXETER, 1836.

# TO MY SISTER, CAROLINE.

My sister dear, and must thou go?
   And will they tear thee thus away?
I ask not now for days—oh! no;
   I ask thee but an hour to stay.

It will relieve the sting of pain;
   'Twill give me yet an hour of bliss;
And, when our hearts are rent in twain,
   How fondly shall I cherish this!

Speak not; I read thy thoughts aright;
   I see thy bosom sink and swell;
Fast gushing tears obscure my sight;—
   The hour has come—to say farewell.

1837.

## TO THE SAME.

And we must part.  Ah ! cruel thought ;
    What deeper sorrow can I feel ?
Why, wretched hour, didst thou, unsought,
    Upon us so perfidious steal ?


How can I view the western sky,
    Which we so oft have gazed upon,
Without recalling, with a sigh,
    These happy hours forever gone ?


How can I watch the glassy stream,
    Beneath the moon's resplendent rays,
When, in its soft reflected beam,
    One only image meets my gaze ?

Or how Contoocook's banks along,
    Thus lonely can I roam again?
My mind will saddened memories throng,
    Of all I am, of all I've been.


Farewell, for thou must seek a home
    Far, far beneath the setting sun;
Yet sometimes leave a thought to roam
    To where life's checkered course begun.


Farewell; but should absorbing care
    Permit remembrance to awake,
Let me thy thoughts some moments share;
    I ask it for our mother's sake.


Farewell, and yet I would impress
    One kiss, my ardent love to tell;
But oh! what language can express
    The anguish of a last farewell?


PETERBORO', *August*, 1837.

# IN THE ALBUM OF A STRANGER.

Go little book, from every friend
   A flower of love receive ;
Their varied hues in beauty blend,
   And friendship's garland weave.

Let every name recorded here
   On memory's tablet shine ;
Each word of friendship be sincere,
   Each heart be true to thine.

To all thy fortune, all thy fame,
   A stranger though I live,
These lines to thee in friendship's name,
   A stranger-friend would give.

EXETER, 1836.

## REFLECTIONS.

### For H. P. D.

The blooming summer sweetly sheds
   Its beauties bright, its smiles serene ;
The blushing rose its fragrance spreads,
   And all the fields are clothed in green.
A few short months, and lo ! a change,
   And such a change as chills the heart ;
From hill and dale and forest range,
   Decaying verdure will depart.


So life to us is shining bright,
   Its summer sun already gleams ;
We taste its pleasures, and delight
   To revel in its fairy dreams.

But soon, too soon, these days must pass,
    And all that would our hearts enslave,
Our joys, our hopes, our dreams, at last
    Must anchor in the silent grave.


And what is life?   A rapid stream,
    Where pains and pleasures ceaseless flow;
A transient hope, a fleeting dream,
    A cup of mingled joy and woe;
A dreary vale which pilgrims pass
    To reach the blooming fields beyond;
A moving tale to which, alas!
    Alternate hopes and fears respond.


And happiness, thou fickle child,
    Where is thy long sought loved retreat?
Is it where fortune's sun hath smiled,
    And honors proud ambition greet?

Is it where pride no wealth will spare,
  An idle fancy to amuse?
Oh! no; thou surely art not there;
  Abode of pride thou wilt not choose.


But in those hearts where virtue reigns,
  Which sweet humility possess,
Where piety an empire gains,
  There, there alone is happiness.
What pleasures pure, what joys untold,
  Await a faithful soul like this,
Since death to it can but unfold
  A world of ever growing bliss!

Exeter, 1836.

6

## TO A LOCK OF HAIR.

Yes, sacred lock, and dost thou sigh,
  The fair one's temples still to deck?
Still graceful on her brow to lie,
  Or float in ringlets round her neck?


I blame thee not; for she is fair
  As angel form in realms above;
She guarded thee with tender care,
  And gave thee all a parent's love.


She taught thee every pleasing grace,
  That her quick eye had learned so well,
And twined thee in the sweet embrace
  Of flowers whose fragrance o'er thee fell.

And thou, amidst the mazy dance,
  Where youth and pleasure joyous meet,
Didst smile at each approving glance,
  That seemed her fairy form to greet.


And oft upon her temples fair,
  When darkness bathed her eyes in sleep,
Thou didst, with grateful love and care,
  Unwearied vigils o'er her keep.


But now, within a narrow cell,
  Which her fair hands for thee have wrought,
Thou dost a lonely captive dwell:
  Such change a single hour has brought.


Oh! never may such be the lot
  Of her who doomed thee thus to pine;
E'en though her beauty be forgot,
  And all her graces cease to shine.

Yes, sacred gift, with pious care
   I'll keep thee for the giver's sake;
That friendship only would I share,
   Whose silken cords can never break.

Such, lady, is the love I claim,
   And such I deem mine own should be;
Though near or distant still the same,
   In friendship constant yet to thee.

GRAFTON, 1838.

# AN ALBUM.

## Fanny Jane Hopkins.

Motto.—*Onward, upward, heavenward.*

Onward, fair motto for a mind
  Conscious of its heavenly birth;
Onward and onward still to find
  New beauties spread o'er all the earth;
And when life's golden sun shall set,
Eternal progress waits it yet.


Upward the willing soul will rise,
  With nature's promptings for its guide;
Aspire to reach its native skies,
  In God's own bosom to abide;
And deem itself no more a whole
Thus linked to the eternal soul.

6*

But heavenward revelation points,
　　And bids us seek the narrow way;
With holy oil the soul anoints,
　　And gilds it with a heavenly ray;
And, in the Saviour's holy name,
It bids us angel-pleasures claim.


Then "onward, upward, heavenward," still,
　　Soar like the eagle to his nest;
Thy mind with heavenly wisdom fill,
　　Thy soul in radiant beauty vest;
And when thou bid'st the world good-night,
Thou, too, shalt bathe in heaven's own light.

CAMBRIDGE, 1838.

## MORAL STRENGTH.

I oft have seen the blooming rose,
   Hard struggling to withstand
The unrelenting gale that blows
   Destruction o'er the land ;
But, rising when the storm was o'er,
It looked more lovely than before.


So virtue, a celestial flower,
   With vice doth oft contend,
And, like the rose beneath the shower,
   It sometimes seems to bend ;
But when the strife has passed away,
It will a nobler strength display.

Firm and more firm it will appear,
   Each folly to oppose,
When malice, envy, hate and fear,
   In frenzy round it close;
For these, like toil of shop or farm,
Serve but to strengthen, not to harm.

Like lights upon a stormy coast,
   Like stars in midnight drear,
'Twill guide us in our vagrant course,
   Through this dark valley here;
And, with a calm, celestial ray,
Conduct us to eternal day.

EXETER, 1834.

# SONG FOR THE GOLDEN BRANCH.

Tune.—*Auld Lang Syne.*

Haste, brothers, haste, and gather round
  The altar of our choice,
Whence come the soft, persuasive tones
  Of friendship's sacred voice.
    For we, a band of brothers stanch,
      Make learning our pursuit;
    And, gathered round the Golden Branch,
      We'll pluck the golden fruit.


Let misers delve for hidden gold,
  To sordid aims confined;
We seek a treasure richer far,—
  A broad and cultured mind.

For we, a band of brothers stanch,
    Make learning our pursuit;
And, gathered round the Golden Branch,
    We'll pluck the golden fruit.


Let grovelling ignorance plod along
    Her dark and gloomy way;
'Tis ours to seek the lofty heights,
    Bathed in refulgent day.
    For we, a band of brothers stanch,
        Make learning our pursuit;
    And, gathered round the Golden Branch,
        We'll pluck the golden fruit.


And may we so pursue the task
    That we have here begun,
That blessings on our heads shall rest,
    When life's great work is done.

For we, a band of brothers stanch,
  Make learning our pursuit;
And, gathered round the Golden Branch,
  We'll pluck the golden fruit.


Come, brothers, since we soon must part,
  Once more our bond renew;
For we must soon, in sorrow's tones,
  Say each to all adieu.
    But still our hearts shall firmly keep,
      While life goes sweeping by,
    The holy vows that we have made,
      And Friendship's Sacred Tie.


EXETER, 1834.

# EXHIBITION ODE.

Days of our youth ; they glide away
　　Like fancy's fleeting dream,
While pleasure's constant smiles appear,
　　And joys around us beam.
Days of our youth ; though years may pass
　　Life's hallowed cup to fill,
Yet memory's pure, undying ray
　　Shall hover o'er you still.


We hasten on with rapid strides
　　To life's appointed goal ;
But strive with wisdom's holy light,
　　To animate the soul ;

To seek the fount whose limpid streams
    Our thirsting minds invite;
Where knowledge swells the crystal flood,
    And kindred hearts unite.


'Tis virtue's calm, unchanging ray
    That sweetens earth below;
That makes the distant future bright,
    And softens hours of woe.
Then let it shine, a brilliant star,
    O'er life's perplexing way,
And guide us through this darksome night
    To heaven's eternal day.


And still, when thinking o'er the past,
    One friend shall ever claim
The warmest feelings of the heart,
    While glows the vital flame.

Long shall remembrance of his care
　　Our grateful bosoms swell,
Though now we speak the parting word,
　　The solemn, long farewell.


We part, as brothers, closely joined
　　In friendship's holy tie,
While fond affection swells the heart,
　　And sorrow heaves a sigh;
We part, to run our destined course,
　　In bands of sacred love,
To meet, we trust, when earth has passed,
　　In endless joys above.


Exeter, 1835.

## SONG.

### STUDENTS' CELEBRATION.

Birthday of Liberty!
Auspicious morning! we
    Hail thy return;
Day of our country's birth,
Day when the fettered earth
First of thy magic worth,
    Freedom, did learn.

Day when oppression sighed,
When freedom's banner wide
    Streamed to the gale;

Let every heart rejoice,
Proud of our fathers' choice,
And every grateful voice
    Liberty hail.


This is our chosen land,
Here we united stand,
    A towering rock;
By the oppressor feared,
By the oppressed revered,
By heavenly wisdom reared,
    Slavery to mock.


Land of the mighty free,
Refuge of liberty,
    Home of the brave;
We love thy rocky shore,
Thy banner we adore,
Floating so proudly o'er
    Tyranny's grave.

Sun of this western sky,
Rise to thy zenith high
 O'er the wide earth ;
Spread through its gloomy maze,
Freedom's reviving rays,
Till every tongue shall praise
 Liberty's birth.

EXETER, *July* 4, 1836.

# THE INDIAN ASSAULT.

## An Exhibition Part.

High in its orb the sun serenely bright,
Poured down its golden beams of heavenly light;
No zephyr blew, no joyful songster sang,
Nor sound, nor echo through the forest rang.
Peace filled the skies above, and smiling lay
The blooming earth in foliage richly gay.
    Far in the forest rife with human woes,
A little hamlet lay in sweet repose.
'Tis Sabbath morn; its pious inmates throng
The holy aisles and raise the choral song;
In lofty strains, where hearts with lips unite,
They praise, O God of heaven! thy throne of light.
But hark ! what sound, what shriek of wild despair,
Midst songs like these awakes the breathless air?

'Tis heard again—one wild, unpitying roar
Of fiendish shouts, more dreadful than before.
The Indians come! the Indians fire the vill!
From voice to voice is echoed wild and shrill.
The mother clasps her child, turns deadly pale;
Heart-rending shrieks the arching roof assail.
One soft embrace the sire can only claim,
Girds on his sword, and dares the threatening flame.
The holy house pours forth a warlike band,
Who seek the foe, and combat hand to hand.
The war-whoop sounds, the vengeful arrows fly,
The din of battle rends the vaulted sky;
While rising flames with raging fury glow,
And clouds of smoke envelop friend and foe.

The little band a doubtful fight maintain,
Attack, repulsed; repulsed, attack again;
While blasts of wind sweep from the hills afar,
Roll on the flames, and swell the tide of war.
Now deep despair their last fond hope has riven,
For rescue now, they only look to heaven.

But hark! above the battle's deafening roar,

A voice of thunder comes, their courage to restore.
A man unknown darts in to stay the flight,
Exhorts, commands, turns back the raging fight.
He comes, with hoary locks and reverend mien,
Like one from heaven, descending all unseen.
His looks divine their fainting hearts inspire,
To turn once more and dare the hostile fire;
While shrieks, the flames, and his firm voice implore
To make one strong, one desperate effort more.
'Tis done; before the charge the foe gives way;
The man unknown decides the doubtful day.

But oh! what anguish fills their bosoms high,
To see their homes in fiery ruins lie;
While many a son and brother round them lay,
Stretched on the earth to gasp their breath away.
The stranger, too—where has the stranger gone?
There's no reply but echo's answering tone.
He came in fight, departed when 'twas o'er;
They knew him not; they never saw him more.

Exeter, 1835.

# PER ALPES TRANSITUS HANNIBALIS.

## An Exhibition Part.

Jamque Aurora oceanum relinquens,
Et coruscans coelo sub alto, nive
Oppletos spargit gelidosque montes
  Lumine pulcro.

Et cadente frigido nunc Boöte,
Nix, gelu concreto, cacumina alta
Obruens abrupta refulgit late
  Lucido sole.

Jamque fessis militibus labore
Duro, contusisque animos, amoenos
Hannibal monstrat viridesque campos
  Italiae almae,

Inclita Romae altaque moenia armis
Et triumphis; praemia digna, acerbûm
Quae, dicit, fortuna et iis laborum
      Termina dabit.


Atque vix haec ediderat, statim cum
Lubricâ procedere jugo ab alto,
Et viâ angustâ Lybiae superbae
      Agmina densa.


Neve radices manibusque lapsi,
Neve virgulta avio monte in alto,
Eminentes; sed glaciesque nives
      Omnia tegunt.


Jamque fessi titubant; secantque
Per gelu; jumenta hominesque cadunt,
Et volutantes alii in gelu acri
      Supra aliosque

Cum ruina horrenda; aliique adhaerent
Alte concreta in glacie, quasique
Alto suspendent pedibus de coelo, hor-
   ribile visu !


Per fera prolapsi aliique saxa
Saepe perfringunt penitus, per Alpes
Undique funduntur eorum hic illic
   Corpora mixta.


Jamque defessi variis periclis
Et fame, in colles veniunt apricos,
Valibus curvis apud atque rivos
   Castraque ponunt.


Late agros annos populando multos
Traxerant pugnandoque, ubi Hannibal tum
Ut caterva invaderet cum potente
   Constitit urbem,

Et èo procedere coeperat, quum
Antecedens multo timorem acerbum
Fama cum luctu tumido superbae
    Attulit urbi.


Undique ploratus in urbe tota
Moestus exauditur; et undique actae
Matronae terrore ruunt deorum
    Circiter aras,


Crinibus passis; duplices àd astra
Et deos tolluntque manus, et orant
Ut ii Romam eriperent cruenti
    Manibus hostis;


Atque ut aras, ut liberos, ut matres
Tuto servarent; trepidantque; tota
Urbe discurrunt; nec amicum ab hoste
    Cernere possunt.

Haec deus, rex magnus Olympi, at vota
Audit, instructas aciesque nimbis
Et procellis ter dirimit, ter atque
       Intonat alto.

EXETER, 1836.

## BANQUET SONG.

### Sophomore Class Supper.

Tune.—*Auld Lang Syne.*

Hail, brothers, hail the festal hour;
The banquet hall is gay;
Here, plunged in pleasure's lulling tide,
We'll drive dull care away.
Then fill the cup with rosy wine,
Drain every goblet dry;
Swell loud the song of festal mirth,
While circling bumpers fly.

Here laughing youth and pleasure meet,
Here sound the notes of glee;
Let wit and humor lend a charm
To glad festivity.

Then fill the cup with rosy wine,
　　Drain every goblet dry;
Swell loud the sounds of festal mirth,
　　While circling bumpers fly.

Two years have sped since first we met,
　　On silent pinions by,
Whose dreams, bright gleaming through the past,
　　In sweet remembrance lie.
　　　Then fill the cup to by-gone days,
　　　　Drink, drink the sparkling wine,
　　　And swell a louder, loftier strain
　　　　To days of "Auld Lang Syne."

Two years are gone, and half our days
　　Of college life are o'er;
We bid adieu to pleasures past,
　　And welcome those before.
　　　Then raise the choral song again,
　　　　Speed round the bowl once more;
　　　We bid adieu to pleasures past,
　　　　And welcome those before.

No storm disturbs the tide of joy,
 No clouds the sky o'ercast;
In hope we paint the future bright,
 In memory view the past.
  Then raise the choral song again,
   Speed round the bowl once more;
  We bid adieu to pleasures past,
   And welcome those before.

The jovial banquet now must close,
 The festive hours have sped;
We part—but yet we meet again
 When two short years have fled.
  Then fill another brimming bowl,
   The fullest and the last,
  And louder sing, we meet again
   When two short years have passed.

CAMBRIDGE, 1837.

# SONG FOR CLASS DAY.

## HARVARD UNIVERSITY.

We meet while grief each bosom swells,
  That late but pleasure knew,
To hear the prayers of those we love,
  And bid a kind adieu.
    We meet—to part at manhood's call,
      When youth's fond dream is o'er;
    When life's young joys are all behind,
      Its mysteries before.


And well may sorrow fill the heart,
  A tear the eye confess,
As now we leave the haunts we've loved,
  And friendship's fond caress;

8*

As now we leave the mates our hearts
Have cherished long and well;
As to the joyous scenes of youth,
We say at last farewell.

Four years—how long and dark they seemed
When early youth looked on,
And yet how soon their tale is told,—
They will be, they are gone;
Gone like the dew-drop from the flower,
Like summer's tinted bow,
Like fancy's dream at twilight hour,
Like angels come below.

Here other voices will be heard,
Here other feet will tread,
While we, by fortune's varying star,
O'er life's dark sea are led.
Farewell, ye groves, which summer winds
Still murmur lightly through;
Farewell, ye halls, where oft we've met,
Ye classic walks, adieu.

Now, classmates—ah ! how many tales
  That single word can tell—
Come, clasp a brother's proffered hand,
  His blessing claim, farewell.
    Farewell, and though we meet no more
      Till life's last link is riven,
    We'll raise above one heartfelt prayer,
      To meet again in heaven.

JULY 18, 1839.

# THE WRECK OF THE ADELINE.

Far on the ocean's restless tide
    A gallant vessel lay;
Her lagging sails hung loose, her side
    Scarce felt the wild waves play;
The winds were hushed, and near and far
The angry waters ceased to war.


But see, far o'er the sunset sea,
    Dark, threatening clouds appear;
They rise, they rise convulsively,
    As if a storm were near;
And now the ocean's distant roar
Proclaims the wind-god loose once more.

The seamen view the threatening skies,
    And furl each dangling sail;
They watch with well-experienced eyes
    The coming of the gale;
And think, as billows round them foam,
Of friends beloved, their own sweet home.

The wind sweeps on resistless now;
    The slumbering waters wake;
The billows rush from stern to prow;
    The proud masts creak and break;
The bark sinks deep, deep in the wave,
And o'er her still the billows rave.

But ah! the seamen, where are they?
    Ask of the wave that floated near;
No tidings will the winds convey
    To a wife's or a loved one's ear;
Yet doth their very silence tell
That deathful tale as true and well.

SCITUATE, 1838.

# SONG FOR NAUSHON.

AIR.—*Sweet Vale of Avoca.*

From the dust of the city, the noise of its streets,
From the warehouse, the pulpit, and college retreats,
The merchant, the parson, the student has come,
O'er smiling Naushon for a season to roam.

And beauty comes too, with her bright beaming face,
With her smiles and her sweetness each pleasure to
    grace,
To watch, from the hill-top, the sky and the sea,
As clouds move majestic and billows roll free.

And the Governor gives to each pleasure a zest,
By his flashes of wit or a well-pointed jest;
He has welcomed us all, with a hearty good will,
To his realm 'midst the waters, his home on the hill.

Less bright is the sun when he sinks in the west,

And folds his proud mantle of gold o'er his breast,

Less lovely the richest drawn tint of the sky,

Than the clear light that flashes in woman's soft eye.


Less free is the deer that bounds gaily along,

Less blithe is the lark as she carols her song,

Than the minds and the hearts of the party upon

The beautiful island of merry Naushon.


Inspired by its beauty, so free and so gay,

We'll laugh and we'll sing all our sorrows away;

We'll roam through the forest, or sail by the shore,

Bidding care to depart and molest us no more.


NAUSHON, *July,* 1839.

# SWORD-FISHING SONG.

Our sails are up, the breeze is fair,
   The light waves round us play,
And through the brine the cup-fish shine
   In beams of early day.
We leave the tranquil bay behind,
   And, far upon the deep,
Through surge and foam where sea-sharks roam,
   The graceful Fawn doth sweep.


The gleaming skies are bright above,
   And bright the waves below ;
While song and mirth to joy give birth,
   Our hearts enraptured glow.

Now watch the surge with eager gaze,
    For here the sword-fish roves,
Whose fin and tail, like mast and sail,
    Betray the path he moves.

See, there in proudest mood he comes,
    Like a fearless warrior on ;
The barbed sea-lance, like lightning's glance,
    Shoots down ;—he sinks, he's gone.
Down, down like leaden weight he goes,
    To yawning caves beneath ;
But through the brine he drags a line,
    That binds him fast to death.

Now man the boats in eager haste,
    The line draw slowly in ;
With failing strength-comes death at length,
    And we the prize shall win.
So tack the sheets, all hands above ;
    No time for mirth or play ;
And soon on deck, a lifeless wreck,
    The armed monarch lay.

9

And there in all his pride he lies,
  With sword so sharp and strong ;
No more he'll roam through sea and foam,
  The coral groves among.
Then back to fair Naushon, my boys,
  With joyous hearts, and gay ;
Let toast and wine with song combine
  To close the merry day.

NAUSHON, *July,* 1839.

# SONNET.

In youth's fair morn, when life is new,
  And the young, joyous heart beats high
  With hope and love; and sorrows fly
Afar, and vanish like the early dew,
When day's star comes, with smiles, to woo
  It upward, danger still is nigh,
  Though all concealed; for flattery,
With lying breath is there, the hue
Of ruddy health to change, and o'er
The mind a sickly paleness spread,
  The heart and giddy brain to store
With all that youth should shun to wed.
  My friend, still lovely as before,
  Through every path of life be led.

1839.

# PETERBORO' ACADEMY.

## DEDICATION ODE.

We meet no pageant train to view,
  In idle pomp displayed,
No crowns to weave, no garlands twine,
  A victor's brow to shade;
But oh! we meet with holier thoughts,
  A nobler sight to see,
We meet to-day to consecrate
  This temple, truth, to thee.


No classic walks are here to tell
  Their many tales of yore;
No ancient grove or time-worn rocks,
  With memories clustered o'er;

Oh ! no; but here in native strength,
   The forest green is spread,
Through whose tall trees this holy spire
   In triumph lifts its head.

As o'er its roof, high throned in clouds,
   The storm-beat branches wave,
And near its base the wooded earth,
   Soft flowing waters lave ;
So may'st thou o'er the youthful mind,
   Proud science, stretch thy sway ;
And so may knowledge deep and clear,
   Wash error's seeds away.

May gifted youths and maidens bright,
   From valley, hill, and plain,
Come here to drink at learning's fount,
   And truth immortal gain ;
And may they here, by science led,
   All mysteries explore,
And with the wisdom of the past,
   The memory richly store.

9*

And long may those, whose liberal hands
　　Have reared this sacred shrine,
Rejoice to see it thus fulfil
　　Its ministry divine;
And may it send, each coming year,
　　With youth's high hopes elate,
A band to be the pulpit's pride,
　　The pillars of the State.

AUGUST, 1837.

# CENTENNIAL ODE.

## Peterboro' N. H., 1839.

Through devious ways and paths unknown,
  Through forests dark and drear,
Our fathers sought these mountain streams,
  To plant their offspring here.

They came not forth from princely halls,
  To wasting pleasures sold;
They came not as the Spaniard came,
  To seek for mines of gold.

But, strong in purpose, high in soul,
  In virtue armed secure,
They came from homes affection blessed,
  They sought for homes as pure.

Through years of toil, through years of want,
  They bravely struggled on,
And lo ! the forest melts away,
  The prowling wolf is gone.


Their flocks increase, and fields of corn
  In summer breezes wave,
And plenty crowns the smiling board,
  When winter tempests rave.


And soon, while busy life flows on,
  And hardship slowly flies,
They see on fair Contoocook's banks
  Their pleasant hamlets rise.


Their names are left for us to bear ;
  Their spirits—they are fled ;
And yon lone hill has gathered in
  The harvest of their dead.

Their homes, their graves may be forgot,
  And yet they will be blessed,
So long as we, their sons, shall own
  The spirit they possessed.

BALTIMORE, 1839.

## SOLDIERS' MONUMENT.

### DEDICATION ODE.

Beside the river's rippling tide,
 The green wood arched above,
To our brave dead we consecrate
 This monument of love;—

To men who, when the thunder shock
 Of war burst o'er the land,
With patriot zeal left all to join
 The nation's mustering band;—

To men who, fired by country's love,
 Flung her proud flag on high,
And dared, to stay the traitor's arm,
 Beneath that flag to die.

Some lie by broad Potomac's flood;
　　One near Antietam moulds;
Some sleep by James; the crater some
　　In its dark bosom holds.

On southern fields, in storms and floods,
　　In swamps with noxious breath,
By battle's shock or fever's heat,
　　They met a soldier's death.

Brave souls! to you we rear this pile,
　　To you, who nobly gave
Your lives, a willing sacrifice,
　　Your country's life to save.

Long may it grace our village grove,
　　Long tell from sire to son,
That death for right is never death,
　　But life immortal won.

Peterboro', 1870.

## ORDINATION HYMN.

O ! thou, whose love our fathers did inspire,
　　To rear, in faith, this temple large and free,
Fill this young heart with all a prophet's fire,
　　And build in us an altar worthy thee.

Teach him to speak thy counsel boldly here,
　　To guide, exhort, encourage, and reprove;
With fervent zeal, and yet with reverent fear,
　　Pronounce thy judgments and proclaim thy love.

Grant him and us thy spirit's quickening power,
　　Plant our firm faith on Christ, the living rock;
In joy and doubt, in sorrow's weary hour,
　　Bless thou and help the shepherd and the flock.

BALTIMORE, 1873.

# TO SIDNEY.

I've loved thee when the summer's sun
  Poured its full radiance down ;
I've loved thee when the spring was young,
  When autumn's leaves were brown.

I've loved thee when the streams were bound
  In winter's icy chain,
And when the sun in Taurus rides
  To bid them leap again.

I've loved thee, and I love thee still ;
  But words, how poor are they,
To tell the love, the glowing love
  That fills my heart to-day.

BALTIMORE, 1846.
10

## TO PRISCILLA,

ON RECEIVING A BALL OF COTTON TWINE, WITH
SOME VERSES ON NORTH AND SOUTH.

The cotton sure is Southern grown,
　　And she who sent it too;
But not the less beloved she,
　　That in the South she grew.


Her heart may glow with Southern pride;—
　　Her grace is all her own;
Her taste, and skill, and strength of will
　　Are culled from every zone.


The South may rear the cotton boll;
　　The North may make the twine;
But love, and faith, and tenderness
　　Will North and South combine.

A daughter's winning look and smile,
   Wherever she may dwell,
Will ever bind a parent's heart
   With chains invincible.

CHRISTMAS, 1886.

# TO MY BIBLE.

## By S. B. M.

Guide of my life, to thee I look
   For comfort and for peace;
Thou art the holy, blessed book
   Whose beauties never cease.

In youth, when snares around me lie
   To tempt my wandering feet,
If thou, my faithful friend, art nigh,
   I safe these dangers meet.

When sickness shakes my feeble frame
   And age has dimmed my eye,
And He, from whom my spirit came,
   Warns me that I must die;

Oh ! then, if I have followed thee,
And safely kept thy word,
How joyful will the summons be
To meet my father, God !

1840.

www.ingramcontent.com/pod-product-compliance
Lightning Source LLC
Chambersburg PA
CBHW032112010726
47493CB00008B/2550